RAINTREE
SCIENCE ADVENTURES

VOLCANOES

Judith E. Greenberg and Helen H. Carey
Illustrated by Charles Shaw

RAINTREE
STECK-VAUGHN
LIBRARY
Austin, Texas

To Bobbi, Rick, Gary, and Eric — **J.G.**
To Helen D. — **H.C.**

Editorial
Barbara J. Behm, Project Editor
Judith Smart, Editor-in-Chief

Art/Production
Suzanne Beck, Art Director
Kathleen A. Hartnett, Designer
Andrew Rupniewski, Production Manager
Eileen Rickey, Typesetter

Reviewed for accuracy by:
Gretchen M. Alexander, Executive Director
West 40 Educational Service Center Number 5
Northlake, Illinois

Scott R. Welty, Instructor
Maine East High School
Park Ridge, Illinois

Library of Congress Number: 89-78284

3 4 5 6 7 8 9 96 95 94 93 92

Library of Congress Cataloging-in-Publication Data

Greenberg, Judith E.
Volcanoes / by Judith E. Greenberg and Helen H. Carey; illustrated by Charles Shaw.
(Raintree science adventures)
Summary: Describes several volcanoes in different areas of the world, the causes and stages of eruption, and potential benefits of volcanoes. 1. Volcanoes—Juvenile literature. [1. Volcanoes.] I. Carey, Helen H. II. Shaw, Charles, 1941- , ill. III. Title. IV. Series.

QE521.3.C36 1990 551.2′1 89-78284
ISBN 0-8172-3756-9 (lib. bdg.)

Before You Begin

This book takes *you* on an adventure to the world of volcanoes! You will see a volcano erupt, or blow up; learn about the Ring of Fire; and do an experiment that will help you understand volcanic activity. You will learn about different kinds of volcanoes. You will also find out how volcanoes can hurt people and how they can help people.

Knowing the words below will help you in your adventure.

caldera a giant crater formed by the explosion or collapse of the top of a volcano
crater a bowl-shaped hole
lava melted rock that pours from a volcano
magma melted rock within the earth
observatory a place for watching and studying facts or happenings of nature
vent an opening, especially one serving as an outlet
volcano a vent in the crust of the earth where hot rock and steam sometimes pour out; also, the cone-shaped hill or mountain that surrounds this vent
volcanologist a scientist who studies volcanoes

Now turn the page, and begin your science adventure!

A Hawaiian Volcano

It is early morning, and you are climbing up a steep path to the top of a **volcano.** It is on the island of Hawaii in the Pacific Ocean. Walking with you is your father. He is a **volcanologist.** He is going to take samples of gas near the opening of the volcano. The gas will help him know if the volcano is getting ready to erupt. You will be safe because the volcanoes on the island of Hawaii do not erupt without warning. Any minute now, you will get to see inside a real volcano!

You work your way through the thick mist surrounding the big **crater** at the top of the volcano. You walk across the crater's hardened, black surface. You stop at an opening in the crater floor and look down. Deep inside, you see a burning hot red and gold river. It is a river of melted rock. It boils and steams and causes great heat. The whole inside of the earth seems to be on fire!

A few days later, you go with your father to a volcano **observatory.** It is located near the volcano that you climbed. "There have been many earthquakes around the volcano," says Dr. Grant, who will be helping your father with research as you travel. Dr. Grant is a geologist. He is a scientist who studies the earth's rocks. "The volcano is going to erupt soon," he says.

Before too long, you hear booming noises. The floor of the observatory begins to wobble. You look out the window at the volcano. A fountain of fire shoots into the air from its top. Burning cinders fly. Bombs of red-hot rocks land near the observatory with a thudding sound. Steaming rivers of melted rock pour down the sides of the volcano into the sea.

You are almost afraid to move. "What's causing the volcano to erupt?" you turn and ask your father.

"Inside the volcano cone is the **vent,** a pipelike tube" answers your father. "It reaches deep into the earth to a lake of hot, melted rock called **magma.** Sometimes gases in the magma push the magma upward. It travels through the vent or through cracks in the sides of the volcano. If the magma is pushed high enough, it pours down the volcano's sides, flinging out pieces of rock. When the magma pours out of the volcano, it is called **lava.**"

Dr. Grant says, "When lava cools, it hardens into layers of rock on the sides of the volcano. This new rock makes the volcano get bigger. Some lava is smooth to walk on. Other lava is sharp and rips up your shoes."

A sudden crash makes you jump because you think the volcano is firing up again. Instead, Pele the cat has come out of her hiding place. She has knocked over a collection of lava rocks. Dr. Grant pets Pele until she purrs. He says, "I named her Pele after the Hawaiian goddess of volcanoes. When Pele hides from me, I know the volcano is going to erupt. Other animals often know when an earthquake is coming, too. They are very sensitive to changes in the air and in the movement of the earth. These changes make animals feel restless. Horses will stomp. Cows will moo. Rabbits will hide."

crater
lava
vent
magma

"Look, Dad," you say. "The needle on that machine is moving. Why is it doing that?"

Your father answers, "That machine is a seismograph. It is an instrument that tells us when there is movement inside the earth. By finding the location of the most movement, we can tell if an earthquake or a volcanic eruption is taking place or is about to.

"A tiltmeter is another instrument that we use to find out if a volcano is getting ready to erupt. If magma is rising inside the volcano, the sides of the volcano bulge out—sometimes a little and sometimes a lot. The tiltmeter points out the change in the shape of a volcano."

Later, you sit by the window to look at the volcano while you eat lunch. The volcano is quiet now. Before you peel your hard-boiled egg, your father asks to see it.

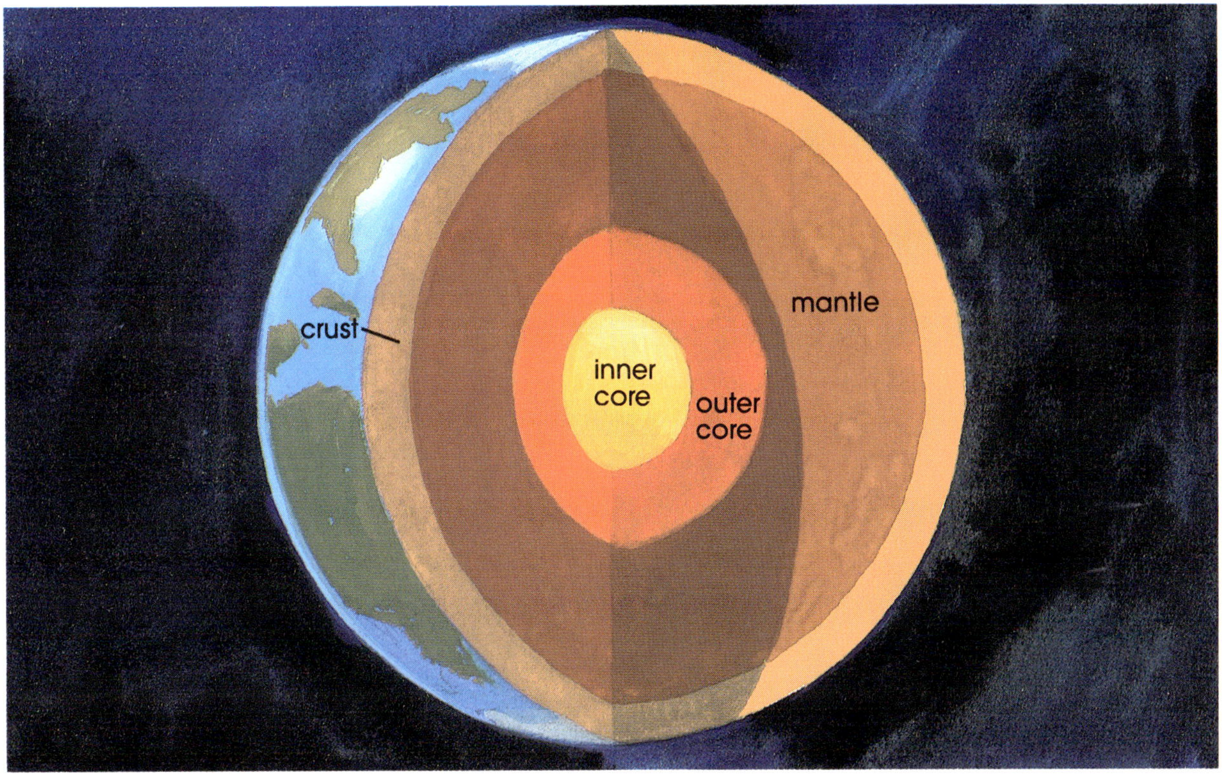

He says, "This egg is a good way to explain volcanoes."

"My egg's a volcano?" you ask.

"Not exactly, but look. The earth is made up of layers. It has a hard, rocky crust like the egg has a shell. The white part of the egg is like the earth's **mantle,** which is also made of rock. The yolk is like the core, or center, of the earth. The earth has an outer core and an inner core. These core areas are very hot."

Your father cracks the eggshell in several places. He says, "The earth's crust isn't one solid piece. Instead, it is made up of pieces like this cracked eggshell. These giant pieces of the earth are called plates. The continents and the oceans are on top of these plates. The plates are always moving, but very, very slowly."

You look closely at the cracked egg. Some pieces of the shell are pushed under other pieces. Others are pushing against each other. Some pieces are pulling away from others.

Your father says, "That's exactly what happens to the earth's plates as they move around. Earthquakes and volcanic eruptions happen when plates are pushing against each other or pulling away from each other. Most volcanoes are found at the edges of these giant plates, often along seacoasts."

Your father explains, "There is a big circle of volcanoes all around the Pacific Ocean. We call this circle the Ring of Fire.

"Hawaii is in the middle of the plate that's under the Pacific Ocean. The Hawaiian Islands are actually the tops of underwater volcanoes.

"There are two other areas of major volcanic activity. One is found where the African and Eurasian plates meet. Another is in the Caribbean Sea. Tomorrow we are going to the island of Martinique in the West Indies. The West Indies are a chain of islands located on the border of the Caribbean Sea."

Awesome Pelée

"You are looking at one of the most violent of all the volcanoes in the world," says your father.

You look up at the giant mountain and shiver. The volcano known as Mount Pelée is the highest part of Martinique. The town of St. Pierre is at the bottom of Mount Pelée.

"While Dr. Grant and I are checking the gases and fissures (cracks) in the volcano, you and Pele can go to the beach," your father says. "You're going to be surprised when you see the sand!"

At the beach, the water is bright blue. The trees are full and green. Much to your surprise, the sand is all black! You dig a deep hole. As far down as you dig, the sand is still black. A girl's voice from behind you says, "The sand is black because the volcano blew up. The ashes from the volcano made the sand black."

You look up at the volcano. "Were you here when Mount Pelée blew up?" you ask, turning toward the girl.

"No, it happened a long time ago. I live in St. Pierre. Everybody learns that the volcano exploded in 1902. In school, we look at pictures of St. Pierre before the eruption and after it. The eruption knocked down all the buildings. It killed all the people except two men," says the girl sadly.

The girl tells you her name is Nicole. You like her. Pele likes Nicole, too. The cat rubs up against Nicole's legs as you walk side by side on the black sand. You pick up something orange that looks like a rock. "It isn't really a rock," says Nicole. "It's part of a roof. The tiles on the roofs in town melted together after the volcano erupted. My teacher said that the side of Mount Pelée exploded. Boiling rocks and mud and a terrible hot cloud of gas raced through the town, burning everything. Even the fish in the ocean died because the water became so hot!"

You look at the giant volcano. You wonder if Mount Pelée is dead or only "sleeping." Your father has told you that sleeping, or quiet, volcanoes are called dormant. You wonder if Mount Pelée will wake up someday and blow up again.

Later that day, your father and Dr. Grant come to the beach to see what you are up to. You ask, "Why was the eruption on Mount Pelée so much bigger than the one we saw in Hawaii?"

Your father hands you a bottle of soda. He says, "Let me see if I can show you. I brought you a soda to drink, but let's use it for an experiment first. Pretend the bottle is Mount Pelée and the soda is what's inside the volcano. If you open it now, what will happen?"

You twist the cap off, and the soda makes a little fizzing noise. You put the cap back on the soda.

"Now shake the bottle five or six times. See all the bubbles? What do you think will happen if you take the cap off slowly? What if you take the cap off quickly?" asks your father.

(Write your guess on a piece of paper.)

Soda
Pop

Your father explains, "A volcano is like a bottle of soda, except the volcano has bubbles of very hot gas. Shake a soda bottle, and the gas bubbles in the soda join together to make bigger bubbles. This creates pressure, or force. When the cap is on, the bubbles stay inside. When you twist the cap a little bit, the bubbles come out quietly. Foam runs down the side of the bottle. However, if you take the cap off quickly, the soda shoots out.

"In Mount Pelée, more and more magma rose from the lower depths, increasing the gas pressure. The gas came roaring out in a great explosion from a weak spot on the side of the volcano. Instead of soda foam, boiling mud and rocks raced down the mountain into St. Pierre."

When your father and Dr. Grant go back to work, you go with Nicole to see her house in St. Pierre. You can see the volcano from her kitchen window. "Aren't you afraid to live so close to the volcano?" you ask.

"Not really. We have scientists who watch the volcano all the time. If they think Mount Pelée is going to erupt again, they warn us," says Nicole.

You hope that Nicole and St. Pierre will always be safe. Tomorrow you leave for Italy. You are going to see a city that a volcanic eruption buried almost two thousand years ago.

A Buried City

Many hours and many, many miles from St. Pierre, your airplane lands at the city of Naples, Italy. Near the airport is Vesuvius, probably the most famous volcano in the world.

Your father says, "On a summer day almost two thousand years ago, Vesuvius erupted. It buried the city of Pompeii under 20 feet (6 meters) of ashes and lava. Pompeii stayed buried for hundreds of years before it was found again.

"We're watching Vesuvius very closely because we think it will erupt again. Many people live on farms on the sides of the volcano. They would be buried if Vesuvius erupted and they weren't warned."

You walk up and down the narrow streets of Pompeii. With the ashes and lava taken away, Pompeii looks as it did when it was part of the ancient Roman Empire. You look into a bakery and see bread that a Pompeiian baker was making when the volcano erupted. You see a helmet that a Roman soldier wore. You ask your guide why it took so long to find Pompeii.

"When Vesuvius was quiet again, people moved back. They built new homes and stores on top of the old city. After a while, they forgot all about Pompeii," the guide answers.

You look up at the volcano. "Why do people want to live near a dangerous volcano like Vesuvius?"

"When a volcano erupts, it puts minerals into the soil. Fruit trees, grapevines, and tomato plants grow big and strong. Farmers will always come back to Vesuvius."

That night you read about two other volcanoes like Vesuvius. One is Mount Saint Helens in the state of Washington in the United States. The other is Krakatoa on an island in Indonesia. You learn that both volcanoes were quiet for many years. People thought that they would never erupt. However, Mount Saint Helens blew its top off in 1980. In 1883, Krakatoa blew itself to bits.

The noise from Krakatoa was the loudest noise ever heard on earth! Thick dust made up of tiny pieces of glass from the volcano was thrown into the air. This dust blocked out the sun for a while. This made the temperature cooler everywhere on earth for two years. The sun and the moon looked red because of all the dust in the air.

"Look at this wave!" you shout suddenly. "It's higher than an apartment building!" Your father rushes into the room to see what the trouble is. He looks at the picture in your book.

"That's a tsunami. *Tsunami* is a Japanese word for a giant water wave set off in the ocean by an earthquake or a volcano," your father says. "When Krakatoa blew up, it left a hole in the ocean. Water rushed in to fill the hole. The movement of the water started the tsunami wave. The Krakatoa tsunami washed away 165 villages and killed 36,000 people."

Pele is snoozing at the foot of your bed. When you close the book about volcanoes, the noise makes Pele jump. She leaps right in the middle of your pillow. You pick her up and look at the big dent in your pillow. "Oh, look, Pele made a crater. Some volcanoes have craters, too. Where do they come from?" you ask.

"Vesuvius and Mount Saint Helens have craters that were formed by eruptions," your father replies. "Crater Lake in Oregon, where we went fishing last year, fills a giant crater. Scientists call a giant crater a **caldera.**

"When magma is blown out of a volcano's vent, there are fewer rocks left inside to hold up the mountain. This can cause the mountain to cave in on top. The top of the volcano will no longer come to a point. It will look like a big cereal bowl. Crater Lake is like a giant bowl filled with melted snow and rainwater."

The Lighthouse of the Mediterranean

The next day, you travel by boat to the island of Stromboli in the Mediterranean Sea. On the island is a volcano that is also called Stromboli. The sea is calm, and you and your father want to go exploring. Late in the afternoon, you talk to the owner of some rowboats. He lets you and your father borrow one for a while. You start to row. You only go a short way when the man yells, "Don't get lost!"

You wonder how you could get lost when all you have to do is keep Stromboli in sight.

You see a big sea turtle, and you and your father follow it for a while. Suddenly, you feel your stomach get tight. A big, black storm cloud is coming. You are afraid.

You are too far out at sea to turn back before the storm hits. All you can do is hold on and see what the storm will do.

The boat bobs and bounces around in the waves and wind. Several hours go by. When the storm finally ends, it is dark outside. You can see the stars. You are out of sight of the island. Which way are the shore and the boathouse? How do you get back?

You and your father watch the sky. You see a glowing light. You wonder what it is.

Then you remember something that your father once told you about Stromboli. The volcano erupts often. However, the eruptions aren't big. They are little ones that throw hot lava into the air. At night, the glow from the lava can be seen for miles! The volcano's glow guides you back to the island.

"That's why Stromboli is called 'The Lighthouse'," your father says later. He then explains the difference between Stromboli and Vesuvius.

"The magma below Stromboli does not explode like a cannon the way that the magma under Vesuvius did and will again. Instead, Stromboli spits out smaller amounts of lava about once every twenty minutes. It continually gets rid of the gas pressure inside of it. A volcano like Vesuvius remains quiet for many years. Pressure inside of it builds for the next huge blast."

A New Volcano Appears!

You continue your adventure by flying to the island country of Iceland. You look out of the airplane windows. It is a clear winter day. On your left, the ground is a flat, white plain. On your right, a big black pile of something is partly covering a house. "What is that black stuff?" you ask.

Your father explains, "The black material is lava and ashes. It once covered about half of this little town in Iceland. About fifteen years ago, a crack in the earth opened. A new volcano formed and erupted."

"What happened to the people when this new volcano erupted?" you ask.

"The people had to leave the island for a while. When they came back, some of their houses were buried in lava and ashes. They had to work very hard to clear the mess away.

"The big, black pile couldn't all be cleared away. Someday, there will be a pasture on top of it. The minerals in the lava and ashes will help make the soil rich."

You think about the pasture that will grow because of the volcano. "Do volcanoes do other good things?" you ask your father.

The Good Side of Volcanoes

There is steam inside of the earth because hot magma heats underground water. Pipes carry this steam into houses and other buildings for heat. Food is grown in greenhouses heated by volcanic steam. In fact, towns are heated by volcanic steam. Volcanic steam also generates electricity to run machines.

Volcanic eruptions bring minerals from deep underground to the surface of the earth. Sulfur is one of these minerals. Sulfur is used in making matches, tires, medicines, and other useful things.

The minerals created by eruptions include metals and gems. Lava with lots of air holes in it is called pumice. Pumice is used to make soap, toothpaste, and cleansers. Ground-up lava can also be used in different ways, such as in the manufacturing of lightweight cement.

On the last day of your volcano adventure, you go swimming in a warm, steamy outdoor pool. Around you are ice-covered trees and snow. The pool has warm water because of the volcano. Volcanic steam is piped under the pool, making the water in the pool wonderful for swimming in Iceland—not just on mild days, but on cold winter days, too!

You know that a volcano can be used to heat homes and run machines. Maybe you could be the one to discover how to use the energy of a volcano to help people in other ways.

What kind of science adventure would you like to go on next?